Septimus Bean and
His Amazing Machine

Quin-Harkin, Janet
Points:0.5 Lvl:2.7

SEPTIMUS BEAN AND HIS AMAZING MACHINE

To librarians, parents, and teachers:

Septimus Bean and His Amazing Machine is a Parents Magazine READ ALOUD Original — one title in a series of colorfully illustrated and fun-to-read stories that young readers will be sure to come back to time and time again.

Now, in this special school and library edition of *Septimus Bean and His Amazing Machine,* adults have an even greater opportunity to increase children's responsiveness to reading and learning — and to have fun every step of the way.

When you finish this story, check the special section at the back of the book. There you will find games, projects, things to talk about, and other educational activities designed to make reading enjoyable by giving children and adults a chance to play together, work together, and talk over the story they have just read.

For a free color catalog describing Gareth Stevens' list of high-quality books, call 1-800-341-3569 (USA) or 1-800-461-9120 (Canada).

Parents Magazine READ ALOUD Originals:

Golly Gump Swallowed a Fly
The Housekeeper's Dog
Who Put the Pepper in the Pot?
Those Terrible Toy-Breakers
The Ghost in Dobbs Diner
The Biggest Shadow in the Zoo
The Old Man and the Afternoon Cat
Septimus Bean and His Amazing Machine
Sherlock Chick's First Case
A Garden for Miss Mouse
Witches Four
Bread and Honey

Pigs in the House
Milk and Cookies
But No Elephants
No Carrots for Harry!
Snow Lion
Henry's Awful Mistake
The Fox with Cold Feet
Get Well, Clown-Arounds!
Pets I Wouldn't Pick
Sherlock Chick and the Giant
  Egg Mystery

Library of Congress Cataloging-in-Publication Data

Quin-Harkin, Janet.
    Septimus Bean and his amazing machine / by Janet Quin-Harkin ; pictures by Art Cumings. — North American library ed.
    p. cm. — (Parents magazine read aloud original)
    Summary: Septimus Bean has built an amazing machine, but its use has yet to be discovered.
    ISBN 0-8368-0887-8
    [1. Inventions—Fiction. 2. Stories in rhyme.] I. Cumings, Art, ill. II. Title. III. Series.
    PZ8.3.Q47Se 1993
    [E]—dc20   92-27110

4/96

This North American library edition published in 1992 by Gareth Stevens Publishing, 1555 North RiverCenter Drive, Suite 201, Milwaukee, Wisconsin 53212, USA, under an arrangement with Parents Magazine Press, New York.

Text © 1979 by Janet Quin-Harkin. Illustrations © 1979 by Art Cumings. End matter © 1992 by Gruner + Jahr, USA, Publishing/Gareth Stevens, Inc.

Printed in the United States of America

1 2 3 4 5 6 7 8 9 98 97 96 95 94 93

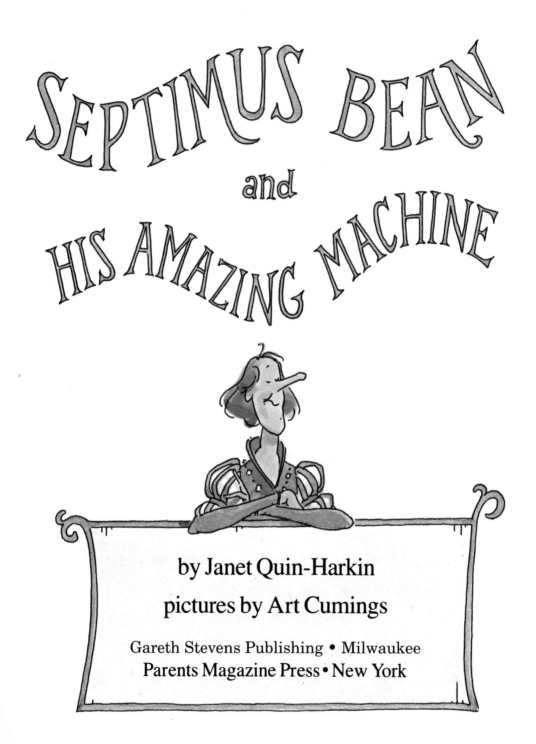

SEPTIMUS BEAN
and
HIS AMAZING MACHINE

by Janet Quin-Harkin

pictures by Art Cumings

Gareth Stevens Publishing • Milwaukee
Parents Magazine Press • New York

To my parents
—J. Q.-H.

Back in the days of King Albert the Third,

there arrived at the palace (as maybe you've heard)

a strange-looking man who was both long and lean.

He went by the name of Septimus Bean—

and he came with a strange and amazing machine.

It was terribly long, and incredibly high,

and it seemed (from the ground) to reach up to the sky.

It had wheels. It had bells. It was painted bright blue.

But King Albert asked, "Septimus, what does it DO?"

11

So Septimus pulled on a huge, heavy switch.

The machine gave a rumble, a choke, and a twitch.

Wheels started to spin, belts started to run,

and steam valves shot off with a noise like a gun.

Flags waved in the breeze, all the gears took to churning,

cog wheels kept turning. . .and turning. . .and turning.

The whole machine shook with a horrible shake.

But the King just asked, "Septimus, what does it MAKE?"

Then Septimus bowed and he answered quite slow:

"I regret, good King Al, that I don't rightly know.

I'm sure it is useful one way or another,

but what it can do I've yet to discover."

Then in rushed the Queen, Petronella by name,
crying, "Children, see here, what a lovely new game!
What is it, my dear?" she asked of the King.
"We're not really sure WHAT to do with the thing,"
said King Albert the Third. "It's use is not clear."
Have you any brilliant suggestions, my dear?"

"Perhaps it cleans floors with that long, funny hose
that looks quite a lot like an elephant's nose,"
said the Queen. "It would save us some time on our chores
if we used it instead of a broom to sweep floors."
So the King nodded over to Septimus Bean,
who pulled out the hose and turned on the machine.

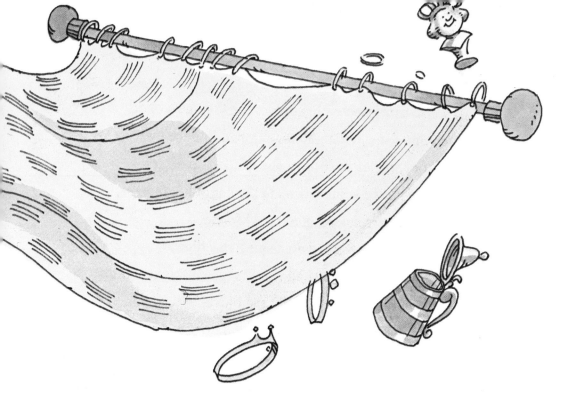

A great blast of air came out with a WHOOSH—
and a tapestry sailed off the wall with a SWOOSH,
sending statues and goblets and coronets flying
and all of the Princesses running off crying.
"Stop! Stop!" cried the Queen as she flew down the room.
"I'd rather sweep floors by myself . . . with a broom!"

Then sweet Princess Primrose, the youngest of all
the King's seven daughters, skipped into the hall.
She took one close look—she needed no other—
and whispered some words in the ear of her mother.
"The Princess suggests to me, Mr. Bean,
that you have invented a washing machine,"
said the Queen. "We shall try this idea of my daughter.
Bring laundry and soap. Fill the barrel with water."
So into the barrel went blouses and dresses
and stockings and skirts of the Seven Princesses.
Then they waited and listened to SQUEAK and to PLOP
till at last the machine slowly ground to a stop.

SOAP
SOAP
OAP
SOAP

19.

As she took out the dripping-wet clothing, the Queen
shouted, "Look! The machine worked! The clothes are all clean!"
Until she saw everything happened to shrink
five sizes too small and was spotted with pink.
"Alas, I don't think, Mr. Bean," said the Queen,
"that this is a truly good washing machine."

Then King Albert grinned widely. He had an idea!
He said, "It's becoming increasingly clear
that this thing has a seat and can move all its wheels.
Let us drive it a little and see how it feels.
Mr. Bean, take your bright blue invention outside.
It may make a fine coach upon which I can ride.
It might go many miles in just one single day
and it will not get tired, and it will not eat hay."
He was all set to start it when up rushed the Queen
crying, "Please leave the driving to Septimus Bean.
Remember, my dear, that you are the King,
and to drive your own coach is not the right thing."

So Septimus climbed up, all eager to please.
He pulled on the switch. The machine gave a sneeze
and a snort and a cough and a bang like a gun,
then it shuddered and juddered and started to run.
"It works! Yes, it goes! Yes, it's moving," they cried.
And the Princesses hurriedly stepped to the side
as it rumbled toward them, gathering speed.
"Now stop, Mr. Bean—we have seen all we need,"
cried the King, but in vain. The machine wouldn't slow.
Called the King with alarm, "My, how fast it can go!
Raise the drawbridge at once before poor Mr. Bean
rushes out and away and is never more seen."

Then the drawbridge rose up to slow down the machine
speeding madly along with poor Septimus Bean.
Up went the machine, never slowing at all,
while the people below held their breath for its fall.
But instead it soared up—and gently it flew,
out over the park as a small speck of blue.

Then the King danced a jig, threw his arms round the Queen,
shouting, "That is the greatest thing I've ever seen!
Who would have guessed that this Septimus Bean
had invented a wonderful flying machine!

29

Bring my coach, get the horses, send soldiers and bands.
We must honor this man when he finally lands."

Then out went the King and his court to the park
and they waited and searched till it grew almost dark.

"What can have become of our Septimus Bean?
Has he flown off to Africa?" worried the Queen.
Then at last came the news—very sad, very grim—
the machine had been found, but with no trace of him.
They rushed to the scene. What a sad, sorry sight!
There were bits of machine scattered left, scattered right.

33

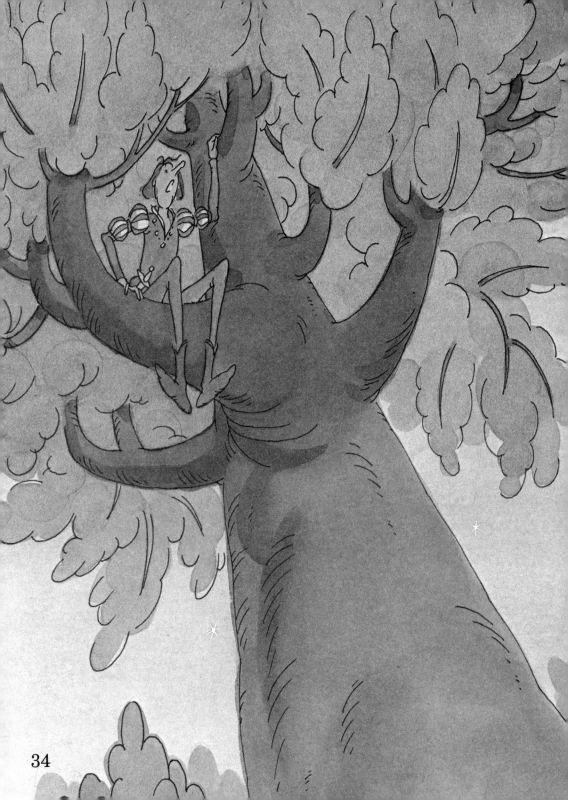

The King stood and looked at the torn-up machine
and he sighed, "What an ending to Septimus Bean."
Then there came a faint voice. (It was too dark to see.)
"I'm not ended, King Al. I'm up here in this tree."

Next morning they went sadly back to the green,
where in twenty-two parts lay the broken machine.
Septimus Bean looked it over, and sighed.
"It's hopeless," he said. And the Princesses cried.
"You'll soon build another, I'm sure," said the Queen.
"You'll fly through the air once more, Mr. Bean."
But Septimus shook his head sadly and said,
"The world must now wait, for I'm going to bed.
I'll never more try to invent a machine.
You can all just forget about Septimus Bean."

But as Septimus turned and walked sadly away,
from behind came the laughter of children at play
and there were the Princesses out on the green
climbing over the bits of the fallen machine.

37

"Look, Mother. Look, Father," the Princesses cried.
"We can swing, we can climb, we can seesaw and slide."

"Come back, oh, come back," called the King and the Queen.
"You've invented a playground, Septimus Bean.
And what could be nicer to visit each day
than a place you've invented for children to play!"

Then the people were called from each village and town
and the King read a speech that was all written down.
"I name this Bean Park. It's a fine place to play
where each child in my kingdom may come any day.
And we all owe this playground to Septimus Bean,
who flew through the air in a flying machine."

THIS PARK IS
DEDICATED TO
SEPTIMUS BEAN
WHO FLEW
THROUGH THE
AIR IN A
FLYING MACHINE

Notes to Grown-ups

Major Themes

Here is a quick guide to the significant themes and concepts at work in *Septimus Bean and His Amazing Machine:*

- the thrill of inventing things
- finding a fun and innovative use for common objects

Step-by-step Ideas for Reading and Talking

Here are some ideas for more give-and-take between kids and grown-ups. The following topics encourage creative discussion of *Septimus Bean and His Amazing Machine* and invite the kind of open-ended response that is consistent with many contemporary approaches to reading, including Whole Language:

- As you read, ask your children to examine closely some of the pictures. In the picture on page 11, for example, can they figure out some of the things that Septimus's machine might be used for? And can they pick out anything special about the usefulness of all the junk lying around in the picture on pages 32-33?
- Ask your child to talk about the many fun things he or she makes or uses from everyday objects around home. Start with kitchen things, such as spoons or pans.

About the Author

Although JANET QUIN-HARKIN began to write as a small girl in England, she wanted to become a lion tamer or an opera singer. After her schooling, however, she wrote plays for the BBC and then managed a rock group.

It is her background in radio that gives Mrs. Quin-Harkin a great feel for how words sound aside from the way they look on a page. And it is in this spirit that *Septimus Bean* skipped off her pen.

About the Artist

ART CUMINGS illustrates both magazines and children's books. "The biggest challenge in illustrating *Septimus Bean*," he says, "was designing the machine so that the pieces fit and made it seem almost like a living thing. Luckily, there were great clues in the story to help work it out."

Games for Learning

Games and activities can stimulate young readers and listeners alike to find out more about words, numbers, and ideas. Here are more ideas for turning learning into fun:

Inventing a Way to Develop Problem-Solving Skills

Children develop problem-solving skills by experimenting with constructions of their own design. With toothpicks and simple connectors, you and your child can become kitchen table inventors, making anything from your own "Amazing Machines" to towers or geodesic domes. There's no "wrong way" to make a toothpick construction, and if left to dry, it can become a permanent creation. You will need the following:

- a bag of *dried* peas, soaked in water overnight.
- one or two boxes of round toothpicks.

To build, simply put a pea on the end of a toothpick and use it as a connector for another toothpick. A single pea will accept two toothpicks easily and can be made to hold more. You may begin by making a triangle, and then extend another triangle off of it so that you are on your way to making a geodesic dome, or make a ladder, tower, or any combination you wish. You and your child may connect your constructions together into one elaborate "machine," create a futuristic toothpick village, or hang your constructions from strings to make mobiles.

Instead of peas, you can use miniature marshmallows, but, naturally, you will lose some of these to nibbling, which is part of the fun! For permanent constructions, peas work better, because the peas shrink as they dry, creating a stronger joint.